ALL THIS HAS NOTHING
TO DO WITII ME

Monica Sabolo is a journalist and writer, and was until recently
the Editor-in-Chief for the cultural pages of *Grazia* in France.
She lives in Paris. *All This Has Nothing To Do With Me*
won France's Prix de Flore 2013.

MONICA SABOLO

ALL THIS HAS NOTHING TO DO WITH ME

Translated by Georgina Collins

PICADOR

First published 2015 by Picador

First published in paperback 2016 by Picador
an imprint of Pan Macmillan
20 New Wharf Road, London N1 9RR
Associated companies throughout the world
www.panmacmillan.com

ISBN 978-1-4472-7497-1

Visit **www.picador.com** to read more about all our books
and to buy them. You will also find features, author interviews and
news of any author events, and you can sign up for e-newsletters
so that you're always first to hear about our new releases.

PART ONE

BLINDED

The first section of our analysis will focus upon the pathological phenomenon 'blind love'. We will see how an individual can be unexpectedly struck down by this tenacious illness, even though that same person has so far been progressing artlessly yet confidently through life. Scientifically speaking it is noteworthy, even poignant, to identify some of the early indicators of the disaster ahead. These intrinsic signs ignite like warnings written in letters of fire, and yet the individual passes hastily by with the innocent smile of a child being led to the sacrificial altar.

The Titanic *leaving Southampton, 10 April 1912*

CRAVAT SYNDROME

Email sent by MS to Alexandra M.
6.40pm, 30 January 2011. Extract.

I think we've found our new editor for the film section.
Remember the guy they said was 'very young and very bright'?
I phoned him, arranged to meet at Café de Flore, and asked
him to bring something I could recognize him by. And he
said, 'I'll wear a cravat.' Don't you think that's rather quirky?
And he did! He wore a cravat! He's tall, looks very young (but
then tries to act older) and he's a right mess. He pulled all
these receipts out of his pockets and he'd scribbled ideas on
them. Absurd ones generally. Then he offered to go to
Pâtisserie Ladurée with me.
He bought a *Religieuse à la Rose.* (Haha – ridiculous.)
I ate half of it.
Obviously, I offered him the job.

Email sent by Alexandra M to MS.
9:28pm, 30 January 2011. Extract.

'I'll wear a cravat'????

THE PHILTRE

Noun. 16th century. Taken from the Latin *philtrum* and from the Greek *philtron*, of the same meaning, derived from *philein*, *'to love'*. Magical potion intended to rouse an intense and fatal passion. 'It was Tristan who inadvertently drank the love philtre with Iseult instead of King Mark, for whom it had been destined.' Definition from the *Dictionnaire Académie Française* (1986 edition).

Religieuse à la Rose, Pâtisserie Ladurée.

Email sent by MS to Alexandra M.
10:28am, 14 February 2011. Extract.

PS. He's been given the desk right opposite mine.
If I stretch out my legs I can touch his feet.

Blinded

Open Plan

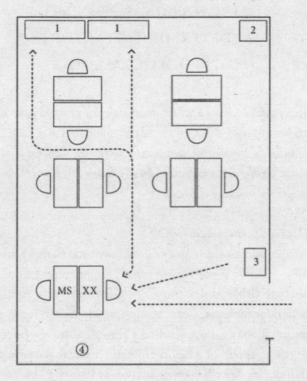

├──┤ 1m

1. Filing cabinets
2. Printer/photocopier
3. Coffee machine
4. Coat stand

---- Regular trips made by XX

PROFESSIONAL PROXIMITY
AS DETERMINING FACTOR FOR
PATHOLOGICAL LOVE

Study undertaken based on data gathered pertaining to the presence of subject XX in the business premises of XXXX Press, situated in Issy-les-Moulineaux, 234 rue du Général-de-Gaulle, Paris, for the period of time: 14 February 2011 to 19 April 2011 (that's 47 working days).

Data collected on subject XX.
Arrives unreasonably late at desk (any time from 11am to 3pm). Chaos. Work station evokes the bedroom of an uncontrollable adolescent. Controlled arrogance. Antisocial behaviour (aphasia, wears headphones so he can listen to music). Looks pale, indicating a chronic absence of sleep and/ or consumption of a blend of illicit chemicals. Accessories indicate membership of a community known to be 'cool': observed wearing a cravat on 39 days out of 47, use of helmet related to possession of Vespa scooter (red in colour), wears SUNGLASSES INSIDE PREMISES.

Parallel data retrieved on subject MS, both positive and negative factors, in other words 'contradictory'.
Problems of metabolism and nutrition (anorexia, bulimia, over-reliance on nicotine). Psychiatric condition (manic

periods [in the presence of subject XX] followed by periods of depression [in the absence (but also presence) of subject XX]. Euphoria. Despondency. Declining levels of concentration. Impulses of an involuntary and obsessive nature (subject MS incessantly contemplates the opportunity of under-the-desk contact between her foot and that of subject XX). Disorders of the nervous system including confusion, trembling, decrease in self-awareness, and problems with speech – e.g. use of word 'penis' instead of 'tennis'. Cardiac complaints (palpitations).

DATA COLLECTION

Email sent by MS to Alexandra M.
9:28pm, 2 March 2011. Extract.

He took me home on his scooter tonight. We had a quick
drink on the way (his suggestion). He must have said about
three sentences. I stole his lighter . . .

7:45–8:30pm, 10 March 2011. Café Le Rostand, Paris VI.

One beer/two glasses of white wine.
Data collected: reckons you can definitively judge an
individual according to his or her five favourite books and
films. Refuses to reply to the question 'What are your five
favourite books and films?' (judged too personal). Is the
author of a 'monograph on Shinji Aoyama' (full of himself).
Split the bill. Physical contact: none.

Blue lighter.

Blinded

8–8:30pm, 14 March 2011. Café Le Petit Suisse, Paris VI.

One beer/one glass of white wine.
Data collected: would love to live in Reykjavik or San
Francisco. Bites his nails. Would like to be the 'man for the
job' as described by Frédéric Berthet in the novel *Simple
Summer's Day* (seems emotionally moved when he talks about
this). Has arrangement to meet 'someone' for dinner. Leaves
MS to pay the bill – no obvious embarrassment. Physical
contact: none.

Yellow lighter.

8:30–9:30pm, 20 March 2011. Café Le Madame, Paris VI.

One Coke/one glass of white wine.
Data collected: has a cold. Claims he doesn't need anyone in
his life. Has a brother, younger (conflictual relationship).
Played the recorder as a child. Rebelled, left his instrument in
a sports bag on a bench on two occasions (stubborn in
nature). Split the bill. Physical contact: none.

Multicoloured stripy lighter.

9–10pm, 23 March 2011. Café Le Madame, Paris VI.

One beer and a martini/three glasses of white wine.
Data collected: was with 'someone' last year (is he gay?).
Knows of Chiara Mastroianni. Quite likes her. Enjoys eating
eels and squid salad. Smiles incredibly sweetly. Physical
contact: none.

Red lighter.

Blinded

8:20–9pm, 23 March 2011. Café du Métro, Paris VI.

One glass of white wine/one glass of white wine.
Data collected: isn't bothered by silence. Doesn't seem to be
aware of companion's state of panic. But appreciates her new
haircut. Remarks that recently he keeps losing all his lighters.
Settles the bill. Physical contact: none.

Serviette, Café du Métro.

MEMENTOS

Alexis M, Geneva, October 1988–April 1989.

Marlboro Red cigarette butts.

Blinded

Gary D, Lausanne, 11 April 1989.

Fork.

David E, Geneva, 1992.

Grey and black stripy woollen APC scarf.

Jérémie B, Paris, November 1993.

Umbrella with two broken spokes.

Blinded

Michael ??, Val d'Isère, February 1997.

Multicoloured ski glove, Le Coq sportif.

THE GIFT

Email sent by MS to Alexandra M.
10:28am, 4 April 2011. Extract.

He gave me a book! (left it on my desk after lunch). The blurb on the back says:

'Frédéric Berthet introduces the hero of *Daimler Departs*: Raphaël Daimler, a detective whose life isn't going too well. But is he a hero or more of an anti-hero? He falls in love, gets dumped, consults Uri Geller who offers to bend a fork for him, then speaks to a psychic who steals photos of his lover.'

Oh my god oh my god OH MY GOD

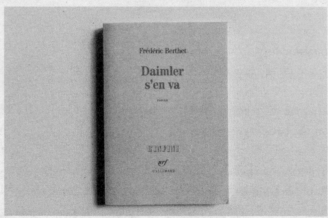

Daimler Departs *by Frédéric Berthet, Gallimard publications,*
Collection L'Infini. Wrapped/unwrapped.

THE LETTER

Monsieur Frédéric Berthet
Éditions Denoël
9, rue du Cherche-Midi
75006 Paris

Dear Monsieur Berthet

I hope you do not mind me writing to you via your publisher. For sentimental reasons that I will not go into, I have recently discovered your body of work. And I must say congratulations, by the way. Unfortunately, *Simple Summer's Day,* your collection of short stories published by Denoël in 2006, is hard to find. I contacted someone in the press office who told me that they do not expect there to be a reprint in the foreseeable future. So, I wanted to ask you a favour. Would it be possible for you to send me a copy of this book? (I will pay you back of course, and please do not hesitate to let me know the shipping costs.)

My request is based on both literary interest (your facetious and melancholic style – seriously, well done there) and psychological necessity. In fact, this text would be useful to me for understanding other similarly overwhelmed and immature young men. Those guys who say things like 'I could be a secret agent' or 'I would like to be the man for the job like in Frédéric Berthet's *Simple Summer's Day*.' What does all that mean? If a man says that, does that mean he is in love?

And don't you think that life is sufficiently draining not to have to search for answers in books that are out of print?

I am very grateful to you for taking the time to read my letter, and look forward to hearing from you in due course.

Yours sincerely
MS

Email sent by Alexandra M to MS.
10:28am, 14 April 2011. Extract.

I watched the clips of Cannes Film Festival. I think I get what you see in him, though I also understand how you might want to give him a good slap – but then I'm probably not being that objective. I couldn't really see if he was losing his hair (I still can't seem to expand the window to full-screen).

PS. Does he ever take his sunglasses off? It was really overcast when they were screening *Les Amours imaginaires* (Imaginary Love Affairs), it looks like it might have been raining.

THE LETTER (FOLLOW-UP)

Dear Monsieur Berthet

I hope you don't mind me writing to you once again. It is because I am in shock, as I have just found out that you have died. Apparently, during the night of 24 December 2003, you succumbed to a cardiac arrest (some sources allude to 'alcohol and depression'). I must say, this news has really got me down.

Not only are you no longer alive, which makes you the archetypal inaccessible man, but also I must admit that I was still waiting for your response, like you would have some kind of revelation for me. Naturally, I am aware that writing to a dead author may appear to be a sign of psychological imbalance. However, I dare say that you will not take offence, what with you being a spiritual man as well as an enthusiastic letter writer (you will be pleased to hear that *Letters, 1973–2003* is currently available from Table Ronde publications). You see, it is apparent to me that despite your recent passing, drafting letters to you could otherwise enlighten me, or at least calm me in some way.

As I told you in my last letter, you make me think a lot about a young man I know, who, if he hasn't already succumbed to a cardiac arrest – his inclination towards alcohol and depression is incontestable – also remains elusive. Do you not think that by putting all this down on paper I could well find answers to my questions regarding this attractive but shifty individual? What do you think? Perhaps you could give me a sign or something: where you are, I am sure you have free time and some writing paper.

All the best
MS

THE INVESTIGATION

Paris–Berry, *Frédéric Berthet, La Table Ronde.*
Letters, 1973–2003, *Frédéric Berthet, La Table Ronde.*
Journal of Truce, *Frédéric Berthet, Gallimard, Collection L'Infini.*
Happiness, *Frédéric Berthet, Gallimard, Collection L'Infini.*

INSOMNIA

'Daimler wakes up in the middle of the night. He slowly opens his eyes and does not move. He keeps breathing calmly. When he is certain it is safe to do so, he gets up and goes to the bathroom for a glass of water.' (Extract from *Daimler Departs* by Frédéric Berthet.)

Glass of water.

THE MYTHOLOGY OF LOCATION

'But when I spend an evening in a more remote district of Paris, as I did several days ago, and I see a restaurant where the local people dine on Sundays, a restaurant where we would not have met anyone we know, I cannot stop myself from thinking about you and adding to the list of places we could have been to. On this planet there is a parallel world, a world where I would have been able to spend my life with Johana, (the world) where I would have been able to fully accept everything that happened to me. You have probably been my only hope of escaping rejection.' (Extract from *Journal of Truce* by Frédéric Berthet.)

Dear Monsieur Berthet

I understand just how you feel! I also have a never-ending list of places where we (the young man you resemble and I) would have been able to go; but also places where he goes regularly, those where he maybe goes, those where I go and where he would never go, those where we went (places that are forever crowned in a halo of light), those where we planned to go, and those where I have vowed to take him, knowing perfectly well that it will never happen. And then, between each of these places, there are streets that flash by as I sit on the back of his red scooter, streets he could zoom up like a fabulous mechanical animal, no doubt those he flies down on his way home, those where I imagine he pulls over before reaching one of these places he would be able to go, those he has no reason at all for driving down but will we ever know? The urban geography and (emotional) transport system are torture, Monsieur Berthet.

MS

OMENS

An omen is a manifestation of the gods for seeing into the future and proves to be a considerable tool for predicting cases of *heart-ache*.

Unfortunately, manifestations of the gods do not occupy the place they deserve in Western society. Hepatoscopy (the study of sacrificed animal livers), for example, proves to be very uncommon in contemporary urban areas.

Likewise, the rarity of flood waters, earthquakes and the scarcity of raptors in built-up areas mean that any observation of natural phenomena is uncertain. In spite of this, any individual who is sensitive to these issues should not lose heart. The tools are there, within easy reach, and by immersing oneself in a state of receptive awareness it is possible to access them. Sadly, the perception of the individual can be distorted for various reasons, leading to an understanding of divine signs only after the fact, when the tragic event has already taken place.

A. THE BEGINNING

Place: Cannes Film Festival

Date: 18 May 2011, 10:30pm–4:30am

Context: *Melancholia* reception, on the 3.14 beach

Soundtrack: *Amoureux solitaires* (*Solitary Lovers*) by Lio.
(only sound data retained.)

Critical moment: 'Don't you want to kiss me?' (request made by
MS at 3:12am in a state of altered consciousness.)

B. THE *TITANIC*
AND PARAPSYCHOLOGICAL PHENOMENA:
PRECURSORY SIGNS OF THE SHIPWRECK

Extract from an article published on the website mondeinconnu.com (author unknown).

10 April 1912: the *Titanic* begins her first transatlantic crossing en route to America. She is a brand new luxury ship that they claimed was unsinkable. However, the shipwreck itself occurred on the night of 14–15 April, a human tragedy that marked the twentieth century and influenced the collective imagination. Bertrand Méheust, the author of *Paranormal Stories of the Titanic*, is interested in the parapsychological phenomena that surround this highly traumatizing event: 'The demise of the *Titanic* seems to have been anticipated or "seen" by dozens of people in England, mainland Europe and the US'. Méheust notes that there seems to have been a huge range of 'unprompted divinatory or prophetic experiences, including dreams, spontaneous flashes of anxiety, and hallucinations experienced in a waking state'.

The World of the Unknown summarizes accounts of these experiences, all of which are practically unknown to the general public. From the very start of its construction, strange stories about the *Titanic* began to circulate. On 31 March 1909, construction began, and the ship received the hull number 390904. One of the draughtsmen realized that this number spelt out the words 'No Pope' when reflected in a mirror. Some workmen believed it was anti-Catholic aggravation and immediately stopped working, convinced that with a serial number like that, the ship would never be under God's protection.

Others made banners saying 'No God, no Pope' which they attached to the hull of the ship whilst it was under construction. A boy who ended up dying on the *Titanic* wrote a letter to his parents in which he claimed to be 'convinced that the vessel would never arrive in America due to the abhorrent blasphemy that covered its sides.' Amongst the workers, rumours surrounding the vessel got bigger by the day: 'the *Titanic* is a cursed ship', they said . . . Around the same time, a number of people who consulted clairvoyants said they were warned about danger relating to a shipwreck. And that was more than three years before the *Titanic* set sail! Then, in the months and weeks preceding the *Titanic*'s maiden voyage, these premonitions increased in number. Many travellers who had already reserved tickets decided to cancel and call off their prestigious journey aboard the Queen of the Seas.

A. (PART 2)
PRECURSORY SIGNS OF THE SHIPWRECK

Now let's go back to section A with a more detached scientific approach. Even as a novice, using parapsychological tools allows one to foresee the catastrophic destiny of the relationship.

Important words are in italics and highlighted in bold.

Place: **Cannes Film Festival**
Date: 18 May 2011, 10:30pm–4:30am
Context: **Melancholia** reception, on the 3.14 beach
Soundtrack: **Amoureux solitaires** (**Solitary Lovers**) by Lio.
(only sound data retained.)
Critical moment: '**Don't** you want to **kiss me**?' (request made by MS at 3:12am in a state of altered consciousness.)

HAPPINESS

Generally happiness emerges in an unexpected way. For reasons that escape all scientific conjecture, the loved one suddenly behaves in a joyful and sentimental manner. His movements are purposeful, he takes the initiative, and while he is set in motion, advancing towards a common goal (the fusion of bodies), the loving one is thrust into a state of treacherous euphoria, somewhere between bliss and debility. Despite the modification of her contemplative faculties, the loving one is overcome by an acute premonition: all this will not last, worse still, all this is not happening. Torn apart by a feeling of imminent loss, the loving one starts to accumulate material proof of her happiness, like plant specimens which lose their colour in an instant when pressed between sheets of paper.

This strategy of preservation, commonly known as *herbarium procedure*, is puerile in nature. Indeed what is more pathetic than a note book filled with sweet chestnut leaves radiating the macabre scent of decay?

A. CANNES

Transcript of text messages.

6:26pm, 20 May 2011, XX to MS.
How's things? Were you at the *Drive* scrng?

6:28pm, 20 May 2011, MS to XX.
A man in the driving seat, seriously hot.

6:28pm, 20 May 2011, XX to MS.
I know this is the tame version, but I was meaning to ask you if you'd like a ride on my scooter. Have you got time?

6:29pm, 20 May 2011, MS to XX.
Yes!

1:42pm, 23 May 2011, MS to XX.
Sorry about the inappropriate behaviour. An uncontrollable impulse.

1:42pm, 23 May 2011, MS to XX.
It must be the sea air.

1:43pm, 23 May 2011, MS to XX.
Are you pissed off? (you just glared at me.)

2:58pm, 23 May 2011, XX to MS.
No.

*Evening pass for the
Nouvelle Vague party.*

Ticket for the screening of Drive,
*directed by Nicolas Winding Refn,
Circle, Grand Théâtre Lumière.*

*Photo of MS taken by
XX in Le Night nightclub.*

Key card for access to a hotel bedroom.

*Map to restaurant Da Laura, rue du
24-Août, Cannes, sketched by MS.*

*Body lotion sample from the Hotel
Palais Stéphanie.*

B. PORTO

On the afternoon of 20 July 2011, XX was playing football and fell victim to a terrible sprain. The scheduled weekend trip to Porto in the company of MS was cancelled. To make up for it, XX organized a Paris/Porto festival of exclusively Portuguese activities staged at his apartment in the 18th district of Paris.

Map of Porto with notes from MS.

The Porto of my Childhood *DVD*, directed by Manoel de Oliveira

The Spousals of God *DVD*, directed by João César Monteiro.

The Phantom *DVD*, directed by João Pedro Rodrigues.

Sleeping with Company: The Second Book of Chronicles, *by António Lobo Antunes, published by Points Seuil.*

Travel kit: toothbrush and toothpaste.

Bottle of Lagrima 'teardrop' white port.

C. LONDON (BRIAN ENO)

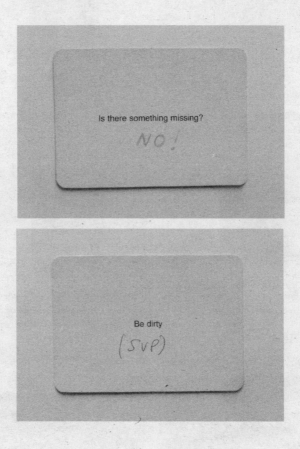

*Cards from the game 'Oblique Strategies
(Over One Hundred Worthwhile Dilemmas)' created by Brian Eno
and Peter Schmidt, given to MS by XX on 12 July 2011.*

PERSONAL DIARY

30 March 2011

This evening we ate at a tiny little Japanese restaurant in the 17th district. The owners, a pair of fifty-something bikers from Kyoto, were approaching our table. XX hardly opened his mouth.
'Doesn't silence bother you?' I asked.
'I'm wary of random chit-chat.'
I smiled. So did he. Then we went back to his and watched the first three episodes of *Freaks and Geeks*. We wore T-shirts, and his arm was around my shoulders under the duvet, like two of the teenagers from the programme.

6 April 2011

This evening we went back to the microscopic Japanese restaurant. I noticed a photo on the wall of the female owner in a leather outfit beside a red and black Honda 500cc. She placed an Asahi beer in front of me. I had the urge to grab her fingers.
He chatted nonstop. He ordered eel. I said, 'Good idea, me too.'
Then we went back to his and watched *Freaks and Geeks*, episodes 4, 5 and 6. I had a panic attack while watching *I'm With the Band* (episode 6). He fell asleep in his white tennis socks.

11 April 2011

This evening the lady owner wore a pair of Converse. She gave me a sympathetic look. He ordered a couple of glasses of sake. I laughed, knocking mine back, and poured myself another.

'I think I'm beginning to like silence,' I said.

'Are you sure?' (mocking me).

I looked at the prawn on my plate, its shrivelled little legs, its little black eyes.

Then we went back to his and watched *Freaks and Geeks,* episodes 7, 8 and 9. I had a panic attack while watching *Girlfriends and Boyfriends* (episode 8). He opened a bottle of Heineken, then the window, in a sweeping motion like you swing open shutters in a holiday home – dubious view, I thought.

20 April 2011

This evening I ate the heads on the prawns. I had a panic attack while watching *The Diary* (episode 10). When we've watched all eighteen episodes what will happen to us then?

DVD boxset: Freaks and Geeks, *created by Paul Feig.*

CATALEPSY

Copy of a note from MS written on an unsealed Treasury Department envelope, deposited on XX's computer keyboard.

Thanks for last night. I don't understand what happened. I'm not always like that, you know. As a general rule, I display an unusual level of audacity and flexibility. Without meaning to brag, I'm a sex machine.
PS: I made myself a coffee, I couldn't find the sugar.

Catalepsy: the complete suspension of voluntary muscle movement in a particular position. The posture which emerges is that of a statue or a mime* artist. A patient in such a state can remain in the same position for hours (whilst a sane individual would be incapable of remaining immobile for so long), thereby giving the impression of a corpse. (Source: fr.wikipedia.org)

---

* *Let's consider for a moment the distressing images implied by the term 'mime'. So the loving one, stunned by the good fortune of having conquered the loved one, finds herself paralysed in this ludicrous way. Fearing that the tiniest movement, the smallest burst of personality might cause the object of her affection to flee, she no longer moves, or at least only within the limits of her biological survival. This deranged behaviour is, in a sadly ironic way, so bizarre and embarrassing that the loving one feigns neutrality and durability. For above all, the loving one does not want to draw attention to what is happening, she even wishes to disappear, to evaporate into the skin of the other.*

Whilst the loving one's personality dissolves, she, utterly powerless, observes the flight of the loved one who, more mobile than ever, cautiously pulls out of the situation.

TELEPATHY

Dear XX, you don't seem to realize that I'm not doing too
well. You are there, opposite me, you write, you type, you type,
you type with those stupid headphones on, but how do you
do it? I'm also writing, you might say to me, I'm also typing,
but believe me, I'm not producing anything worthwhile as far
as work is concerned. You are wearing a lovely cravat, but you
look tired, you're coughing (that ruins your colleagues'
concentration, you know), I bet you went out last night,
didn't you? What a question, of course you went out, like you
do every evening, of course you carried on leading the life I
know nothing about (I imagine you surrounded by pretty
heroin addicts). And me? Well, I slept. I went to bed at 9pm:
ridiculous, but there you go, this affair is wearing me out.
(Though can we really talk of an *affair* when one of the parties
involved spends his nights in shady places and the other
wanders around in pyjamas banging her fist on the bathroom
shelf, muttering, 'That's it! Enough!'? Can we talk of a love
affair as far as we're concerned? Oh! You're blowing your nose.
Can I take that as a 'yes'?)

Your attention please. I'm going to carry out a remarkable act.
I'm going to send you a message by using the simple power of
my mind: Dear XX, we have no past, probably no future,
would you be kind enough to invite me out for a drink this

evening? Could you please stroke your cravat to say you will, a sort of 'roger that'?

A MONTH IN THE LIFE OF MS

Time in the office: 150 hours.
Hours spent with XX (outside work): 35.
Happy time spent with XX: 2 hours.
Time brushing teeth: 2½ hours.
Tears: 4 hours.
Sex: 1½ hours.

THE RUSE

'Still on the subject of the telephone: when Daimler decides to go for broke, he prepares himself psychologically. Then he pulls on his black leather gloves before dialling the number.' (Extract from *Daimler Departs* by Frédéric Berthet.)

Message left by MS on XX's voicemail,
00:12am, 30 July 2011

'Hi there, it's me . . . I am relieved to get your voicemail . . . I just wanted to say . . . I don't know what's happening right now . . . To cut a long story short, I don't think this experience is all that great. Do you know what I mean? It's just not great, is it? . . . I don't want to hurt you, but if it's going to carry on in the same way, it would be best to stop, don't you think? *(cheerful voice, escalating to a high-pitched one)* Maybe we should just be friends . . . Right, hugs and kisses *(cheery tone)*.'

Black leather gloves.

*MISS*FORTUNE

Transcript of a meeting with Maurice P, rue de Paradis, Paris X, 19 June 2011. Discussion takes place after the meticulous observation of MS's palm with the help of a magnifying glass.

'Umm . . . do you travel a lot?'

'Err no, not a lot.'

'I see mountains . . . most likely Austria. Or maybe Spain.'

'I don't like Spain very much. Could it be Portugal?'

'No, there are mountains . . . Austria. There's snow. Do you do winter sports at all?'

'Not much now, not for the last ten years or so.'

'Ahh there you go, these must be images of your childhood . . . (*silently focused*). I see you're going to update your software.'

'Oh.'

'Yes, you're even going to get training on it. Does that mean anything to you?'

'Err . . . No . . . But I really must confess it isn't my main concern here.'

'Yes, but it's there, in any case (*circular hand movements in front of MS's face*). It's imminent.'

'Oh, OK, very good, thank you.'

'I see a boy . . .'

'Oh?'

(*nodding head cautiously*) 'You're in love.'

(*nodding head timidly*) 'Yes.'
(*shaking head anxiously*) 'The outcome isn't positive.'
'What does that mean?'
'Is he married?'
'He's very young, you know.'
(*shaking head cautiously*) 'The outcome isn't good.'

Traditional magnifying glass with black handle.

PHARMACOPOEIA

Transcript of a conversation with Sophie V, pharmacist, City Pharma, rue du Four, Paris VI, 20 July 2011.

'I don't feel very well at all: I'm really unhappy, I'm crying a lot . . .'

'Are you feeling anxious at all?'

'Not really, I'm just very unhappy.'

'Are you sleeping?'

'Yes, yes, that's fine. No, I am just crying all the time.'

'Here, you need to take these. Two tablets, morning and night, and then you slowly reduce the dose over a few days.'

Box of Euphytose,
for mild anxiety and insomnia.

DENIAL

'Daimler has a theory according to which, these days, true romantics are required to pass themselves off as cynics. He refuses to explain further when he's asked about it.' (Extract from *Daimler Departs* by Frédéric Berthet.)

Extract from a conversation between MS and XX, at Chez Ogazu, rue Sainte-Anne, Paris II, 12 June 2011.

'Do you mean to say that the next stage in our relationship is boredom?'

'Inevitably, yes.'

'That's very depressing.'

'Well no. You see, at the moment we're in the emulation phase, and it's a rather pleasant stage. But it's like the Tour de France: each leg can last anywhere between two and a hundred and fifty kilometres.'

Dried fish.

CYNICISM: THE ILLUSION OF BATTLE

Let us pause for a moment to consider the personal perspective described as a *cynical attitude*, a distinctive feature that characterizes the loved one. It is easy to imagine how much this rhetorical art, this supposed rebellion of the mind against over-sentimentality and posturing, puts strain upon the soul of the loving one. The detachment, dry humour and cruelty which arise from it both captivate and blind at the same time. For, as verified by EVERY SINGLE empirical study, the loving one – who we will call 'Romantic' – sees in this feigned indifference the behaviour of a desperate individual. The hopeless mind that characterizes the 'Romantic' works hard to conclude that composure, contempt and cruelty are indicative of an individual who is *on edge.**

Consequently, in a blind desire to see emotion triumph over the world, the 'Romantic' gathers all her strength (which is poor as her energy has been snatched away by nights spent composing embarrassing speeches) and prepares for a battle that will never take place. For the 'Cynic' declines the battle (his skill is that of evasion), though of course that will not prevent carnage as no doubt the 'Romantic' will see her heart ripped apart just like a slab of rump steak thrown into a bear pit.

* *As soon as an individual begins to use terms such as 'on edge' or 'hyper-sensitive' to describe the loved one, human society and the attainment of happiness must be considered beyond all hope.*

THE ENIGMA

We can reflect on deeper – existential – reasons for the loving one's persistent affection for the loved one. We have seen that romantic combat that aims for the victory of emotion over reason constitutes a powerful driving force. But it is a combination of factors that guarantees the longevity of this relationship and offers the loving one the appealing possibility of completely ruining her life and ending her days dishevelled, in a tracksuit, haranguing an invisible voice in the clinical white corridors of a care home.

As well as sentimental hysteria, inactivity and rashness, the loving one's inclination towards *foreign tongues* often overwhelms her. But it is not merely a question of superficial attraction for say a Brazilian or a British individual (there was one from Manchester), though admittedly that sort of attraction is undeniable. No, it is a matter of a penchant towards the *Other*, a hazy concept which encompasses a multitude of metaphysical notions (*The Absolute/ Poetry/Ecstasy/Freedom*), of which the loved one is seemingly Earth's representative. In fact, this representative seems to be the bearer of an enigma: just a few words, gestures, even his simple presence in the world raises awareness of an incredible secret. The loving one, who forges ahead with all this as if chasing the shadow of Grace, is painfully impatient to gain access to this secret, which naturally will never be revealed to her. This quest may not open the door of another world to her, but at least it has the virtue of keeping her busy and diverting her attention from real problems.

Before she left to go on a week's holiday to Tangiers, MS worried about how XX planned to keep in touch, knowing that he hated speaking on the phone and 'like Franz Kafka', was wary of letters. 'We'll find a way,' XX replied.

Selection of photo messages from XX and MS between 15 and 23 July 2011:

2:15pm, 15 July 2011, XX to MS.

3:02pm, 15 July 2011, MS to XX.

10:38pm, 18 July 2011, XX to MS.

2:38pm, 19 July 2011, MS to XX.

3:50pm, 20 July 2011, XX to MS.

4:03pm, 20 July 2011, MS to XX.

7:52pm, 20 July 2011, MS to XX.

3:03pm, 22 July 2011, XX to MS.

RHETORIC

'Indeed, we see many men and women who continue to want to talk things out with someone (or something) who will not understand them anyway, and these people carry on like that, shifting between misery and heroism, as if clinging on to the door of a car when a loved one is departing, leaving, and the car sets off: you are running beside it but of course it is unlikely that you will be able to hold on for more than two hundred metres, depending on the car's speed of acceleration, for some people are very quick when they pull away.' (Extract from *Journal of Truce* by Frédéric Berthet.)

Extracts from notes written by MS in July and September 2011.

'If I'd been aware that it would have only taken a small jolt to rattle you, my pain would have been lessened. No doubt your reasoning comforts you. Nothing has ever seemed more pointless to me, more hopeless than mine.'

'All this sickens me and gives me a chilling sensation because I don't know who you are at all any more. Or rather, I know too well. I don't understand what you are looking for in life. I'm sorry if that's hurtful but I can't put up with it any more (*illegible scrawl*). Maybe it's also what will finally put an end to my affection, at least I really do hope so.'

'mystery/intimate/warmth/shares common breath/I'm mistaken/I blame myself/illusion . . .'

'inexplicable, it escapes us: everything was possible just because there wasn't any space.'

'I don't understand why you're doing this to me. Every time you give me these looks of surprise, or infuriation, I could be hurt.'

'What we're going through is odd, fanciful, poetic, dangerous, uncertain, touching, hot (*last word crossed out*).'

'WE *HAVE* SOMETHNG HERE. SHIT.'

'Instructions for use: an insult, to me, is an admission of sadness, a cry – clumsy though it might be – for a little warmth.'

'You speak foolishly . . . To my eyes, it was your most flamboyant gesture. A highway exit, at last. Be brave be brave.'

'Inexhaustive list of proposals in the hope of getting me back: inviting me to dinner (I refuse), reinviting me (I refuse) and the same every day until I eventually give in. Taking me on a weekend break to Porto; saying hello by passionately kissing me in the open air; taking me to Fontainebleau by scooter with a small Décathlon rucksack on your back (during office hours).'

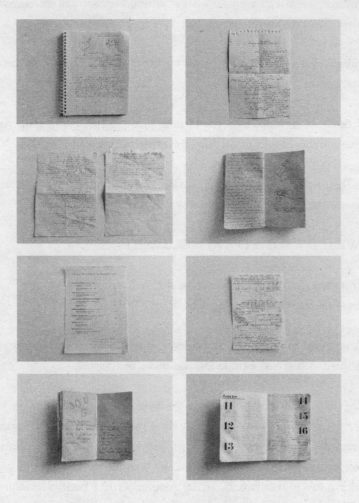

Notes written by MS between July and September 2011. Copies of Alain Robbe-Grillet's broken-heart drawings from his 1950s letter to Catherine Rstakian.

SOCIAL NETWORKS

Facebook France
Customer Services
28, rue de l'Amiral-Hamelin
75016 PARIS

Registered delivery

Dear Sir/Madam

Re: Request for information regarding the viewing of Facebook profiles.

I have been using your services for a short while now, but I have been led to contact you due to several questions that have arisen. Unfortunately, I am unable to find the answers to these by consulting the Statement of Rights and Responsibilities detailed on your site. Therefore, I would be very grateful if you could help me, by any means you deem necessary, to acquire information related to the following three questions:

Firstly, is it possible for a user to be informed about the consultation of his or her profile by another user even if the users are not united by friendship, as defined by your site?

Secondly, can your site alert a user to an abnormally increased consultation rate of his or her profile by the same person? And if so, what are the defined thresholds of abnormality?

Thirdly and finally, is it possible, even temporarily, to gain access to the information available on a particular profile by someone who is not linked to that profile by the aforementioned classification of friendship?

Please do not hesitate to get in touch should you require any further information. I look forward to hearing from you and thank you in advance for taking the time to consider this request.

Yours faithfully

MS

HEPATOSCOPY

Dissection and study of a chicken liver by MS, 3 September 2011.
Inconclusive reading.

Chicken liver.
(Source: Monoprix supermarket, rue de Rennes, Paris VI.)

MOBILE TELEPHONY

Bouygues Telecom
Tour Sequana
82, rue Henri-Farman
92447 Issy-les-Moulineaux

Registered delivery

Dear Sir/Madam

Re: Request for information relating to short message service (SMS).

I am writing this letter to your company to request information regarding your short message service/text messages.

It seems to be a well-known fact that errors sometimes occur in the delivery of the aforementioned messages. For personal reasons, I would be very grateful if you could send me statistics outlining the frequency of this occurrence. Failing that, to what extent would it be possible to provide a document that simply confirms that delivery errors do occur?

In addition, could you could let me know if it is possible to destroy at long-distance an archived SMS exchange in the telephone of a third party whose number is known. And if this is possible, I would appreciate it if you could outline the steps to follow so this can be achieved.

Please do not hesitate to get in touch should you require any further information. I look forward to hearing from you and thank you in advance for taking the time to consider this request.

Yours faithfully

MS

VOODOO

Monsieur Diakgite
24, rue Albert
75013 Paris

Dear Monsieur Diakgite

I take the liberty of writing to you as I received one of your flyers at the Porte d'Orléans metro station, and the caption ('NO PROBLEM WITHOUT A SOLUTION') attracted my attention. I admit that you have succeeded in intriguing me, despite my natural scepticism and the dreadful reputation of your profession. Could it possibly be due to your use of hard-hitting slogans and the simple message of your punchy marketing campaign? Because you see, Monsieur Diakgite, my partner does not run behind me 'like a dog behind his master' – in fact he runs around quite freely. But the idea suddenly seems quite appealing, despite the fact that I have never thought in these terms before.

That is why, as you request on your flyer, I enclose a stamped addressed envelope, a photo of me, my date and place of birth as well as a cigarette butt which the loved one has placed between his lips.

I very much appreciate the time and attention that you will, no doubt, give to this issue.

Yours sincerely

MS

'No problem without a solution' flyer.

PART TWO

PAST HISTORY

AMBRA

When Ambra saw him for the first time in June 1970, she was nineteen years old and wore a kilt and white socks that came up to her knees. She had just left Aiglon College, a Swiss boarding school for girls which combined the discipline of the Wehrmacht with the customs of the European imperial courts. She often remembered the feelings of relief and dread that overcame her when her parents came to collect her in their Maserati that purred like a luxury cat. It felt as if she was being released after a long prison sentence, and yet life was moving far too quickly to avoid complete panic.

Alessandro F appeared to her in a halo of light, like Saint Francis of Assisi. He was sitting on the sofa in the family's apartment in Milan with a guitar on his knees, surrounded by girls playing with their long hair, like seaweed swaying in the waves. She recognized her brother Augusto in the gathering, but he was bathing in Alessandro's blinding light and Ambra was no longer certain that it was really him, as if nothing was quite certain in this world any more.

Two months later, she left the house at three o'clock in the morning with a Gucci suitcase stolen from her mother. Alessandro was waiting for her on the corner of via Domenichino in a Fiat Topolino with his guitar, some works of baroque poetry and general literature guides on the back seat. He was twenty-one, with a little girl and a wife who was three months pregnant.

But his wife and daughter belonged to a world before, a world that no longer concerned Ambra and Alessandro as they prepared to leave at 55 mph on the *autostrada*.

Ambra and Alessandro moved into a small block of flats on via Tiziano in Milan, just a few hundred metres from their respective former lives. (The *autostrada* adventure had been short-lived, both enthusiasm and petrol finally running out.) There she experienced an indecent amount of happiness, despite the hunger, insects, scandal, inactivity, girls with aquatic hair wandering in all the time and letters from her mother that had crinkled as the tears dried.

In December, she found out she was pregnant. He took out his guitar and a bottle of Moscato. She felt as if she was falling into a hole, but most likely it was just the pregnancy hormones.

Alessandro F returned to his wife and his family home at the start of March, just in time to witness the birth of his son, who was named Tommaso without anyone asking Alessandro his opinion. Ambra returned to her parents' place, weighed down by the Gucci suitcase and an extra 17 kilos. In the weeks that followed, she felt like a stranger in this body which occupied so much space so scandalously. With liquid eyes and a deathly pale complexion, she wandered from the bedroom to the kitchen, from the kitchen to the bathroom, without her feet ever seeming to touch the ground. She floated around in a nightshirt, like a voluminous but intangible ghost. In any case, her father acted as if Ambra and her offensive abdomen did not exist, while her mother abandoned the premises, taking refuge in swimwear shops where she dreamt of a new life in Mar del Plata.

On 27 July 1971, at 12:45 in the afternoon, she gave birth at the Grande Ospedale, 9 via Caradosso, alone in a room which reminded her of a prison cell. 'Alone like a dog,' she clarified later. Her brother Augusto came round to see her during the day. She blew her nose on her shirt while glancing suspiciously at Monica, who, looking disconcertingly like a chicken, had been plonked at the end of the bed like an unclaimed parcel.

Eight months later, Alessandro F sent Ambra a gold necklace with a pendant of a little girl with bunches. It was accompanied by a long letter, full of remorse and Latin quotations. She burnt the letter, put the pendant away in a pencil case and went to buy some cigarettes.

*Photo of Ambra
taken by Alessandro F in 1970.*

Gold chain belonging to Ambra,
pendant of a little girl with bunches.

Ambra, May 1971.

Monica, July 1971.

Ambra and Monica, September 1971.

GENETICS

Let's pause for a moment to consider the destiny of this foetus that, unknowingly involved in events that did not concern it, was nevertheless marked by those events, which etched a secret memory on its cells. After the euphoria of conception, it developed its first organs in a peaceful world, a world that felt like eternity. And while it was faithfully drifting in the comfort of the current, suddenly an unidentified cataclysm engulfed it, plunging it into a doleful silence, a Dead Sea in which it seemed to be the last survivor. Its heart was beating, its nutritional needs were satisfied, but the organism to which it was linked by an umbilical cord, like an electric cable, was sending it worrisome signals. Long pulses, then short ones, long harrowing moans, queasy hiccups, acidic convulsions, macabre sighs, increasingly feeble inhalations; before transmissions stopped altogether. There was good reason to ponder existence, for it had begun like a large carnival, then seemingly it was extinguished without explanation, in silent misery.

The issue of the mysterious power of transmission arises here. What do you transmit to your child? Blonde hair, blue eyes, very small feet? But also a taste for cigarettes, panettone, boys with guitars? Is this foetus's life destined to be filled with suitcases packed in the middle of the night, suitcases that will always return to their point of departure some weeks later?

In other words, is this foetus destined to relive, again and again, emotions encoded in a fossilized region of its brain and thus, almost simultaneously, experience love and the end of the world, hope and lightning, a romantic comedy and a horror film?

LEGACY

Study of the transmission of genetic material from one generation to the next.

Data relating to the father has been established by deduction, historical reconstruction or on the basis of witness statements deemed admissible despite the unpredictable independence of thinking with regard to the sources of information.

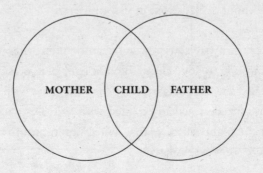

MOTHER	CHILD	FATHER
BLUE EYES	BLUE EYES	BLUE EYES
BLONDE	BLONDE	DARK BLONDE
GIFT FOR DRAWING	/	GIFT FOR MUSIC
BLOOD GROUP A	BLOOD GROUP A Rh positive	DATA UNAVAILABLE
PULMONARY WEAKNESS	PULMONARY WEAKNESS	DATA UNAVAILABLE
STOMACH DISORDERS	ECZEMA, SHINGLES, PROBLEMS WITH BALANCE	DATA UNAVAILABLE
MANIC DEPRESSIVE	LYRICAL MELANCHOLY	LYRICISM
DEPENDENT PERSONALITY	DEPENDENCE UPON ELUSIVE MEN	ELUSIVE PERSONALITY
ROMANTICISM	FALLS IN LOVE EASILY	DON JUANISM
CHRONIC IMMATURITY	CHRONIC IMMATURITY	CHRONIC IMMATURITY
BORDERLINE PERSONALITY DISORDER	NARCISSISTIC PERSONALITY DISORDER	NARCISSISTIC PERSONALITY DISORDER
NICOTINE ADDICTION	NICOTINE ADDICTION	NICOTINE ADDICTION

MONICA

During the summer of 1977, Monica was lovestruck. She spent her holidays in Guadeloupe where she collected shells on the beach whilst her parents took siestas to recuperate from a year of toil and the demands of urban high society. But it was Monica who was more exhausted than anyone else. During the first six years of her existence, she had developed superpowers, a sensory awareness allowing her to distinguish every shift in her mother's mood. Her body seemed to be studded with sensors: she detected the tiniest magnetic variations, tremors in the air, organic vibrations, respiratory rhythms, even her mother's heart beats. Like sharks that detect the electric field of fish in distress, she continually received information indicating maternal instability. She went to school, played with her brother, and took judo and ballet classes (where, incidentally, she stood out through a cruel lack of coordination). But these were just extra-curricular activities. The world revolved around Ambra, this blonde, melancholic creature who chain-smoked and found it harder and harder to get out of bed.

That summer, Monica got to know a boy in red swimming trunks, swimming trunks that he wore on every occasion, including those where they did not seem to be appropriate, like tennis practice or mini-golf. Instantaneously, he inspired a feeling of fear and respect in her. He exuded a remarkable calmness, and his movements were unbelievably synchronized.

He did cartwheels, jumped across rocks, slam-dunked at table tennis, dived backwards into the pool, and 'mimed a sex act' by rubbing himself in the sand. He was seven, and essentially knew life at its darkest and most dangerous, as well as all that related to the anatomy. She did not immediately understand the butterflies that fluttered around in her stomach when the red blot of his trunks suddenly appeared in her field of vision.

One afternoon, when he had lured her into his hotel bedroom by promising that there was a crime scene to look at, she discovered the corpse of a crab on the carpet, its legs twisted, its eyes lying alongside its body like two miniature snooker balls.

She took refuge in the bathroom, reflecting on the dangers of everyday life (the tragedy apparently occurred due to the converging of a pincer and a plug socket), and in turn she also received a fatal shock. He entered the bathroom, closed the door behind him with terrifying determination, and spoke the following words, which consumed her body like flames: 'Kiss me, or you're not getting out of here.'

From that moment on, Monica's movements were no longer controlled by her brain but by mechanical reflexes, a sort of survival impulse, all in slow motion and with a hum that filled the air as though a swarm of bees had moved in behind the shower curtain. She moved forward and while her heart made strange suction noises, she pressed her pursed lips against the mouth of the hostage-taker.

The whole time he kept his hands on her hips like a man who had seen it all before, whilst she clung on to his shoulders with the despair of someone drowning.

The memory of his male authority permeated her nerve endings for ever. Her sin haunted her consciousness but, in the months that followed, she still responded to all his letters, disturbing missives written in pencil on sheets of graph paper. He advised her to hide his letters, worried too about their terrible wrongdoing, but he always finished by asking her to give her parents a hug, which drove her into a state of bewilderment and reinforced the torment.

At Christmas, he sent her a postcard from Crans-Montana, saying that he intended to visit her in Geneva. That was the last time she heard from him. In April, she stopped hoping to see him on the way out of school (in her dreams, he always wore his swimming trunks in the playground, which only slightly interfered with her euphoria). She threw herself at her mother, who was smoking a Muratti Ambassador whilst preparing the breakfast. 'I won't ever fall in love again, it hurts too much,' she announced, while her mother gazed out of the window, in her eyes the distant resignation of an abandoned woman.

ANXIETY

Message written by Monica for Ambra's birthday, October 1979.

'happy birthday mummy,
doing the howswork for mummys birthday
hurying to finish the birthday kake
dont tell anywon your age even if your 29
nowing that she wont like her prezent
I love you lots.'

Booklet created by Monica, 1979.

MONICA (PART 2)

By 1984, Monica had still not kissed another boy. She was around twenty centimetres shorter than the other girls in her class, who wore mascara and looked as though they had progressed to a superior stage in life. They moved around in groups, pulled together by secret signals indicating their membership of a particular tribe of initiates. They flirted with the male species and mastered the secret protocols: Brazilian bracelets, cigarettes in the toilets, cascades of hair rolled up in a band. Monica watched them pass her in the corridors with a feeling of ashamed underdevelopment, a sense of having been betrayed by nature. In the space of several months, they had lost their cheeks and sprouted like tropical plants, while her body was fossilized in a prehistoric stage of evolution, deprived of the attributes which promised to unlock interesting prospects, such as the mixing of saliva or fingers sliding between shirt buttons.

She was sometimes invited to parties, where she moved around cautiously, doing her utmost to appear relaxed and unconcerned by her solitude. She would daringly follow the flow of boys to where they smoked at the bedroom windows, but they were indifferent and wandered away.

It was during one of these lively ordeals that she got to know Lyonel, who, as well as perpetually sweating like a bucket, suffered from a growth impediment.

He was the shape of a sickly child, but his face seemed to have reached an advanced hormonal stage. He had dark rings under his eyes betraying a renal dysfunction, and hair that gleamed like the coat of an aquatic mammal. This surprising dichotomy between his size and the surge of testosterone exuded by his body had a disastrous effect on his social life. Whenever he came close to members of the female sex, they escaped like a flutter of butterflies, sentencing him to evolve on the periphery of existence. It was there, in the wings of the world, stuck at a dining room table adorned with bottles of Oasis, that he suggested smoking a cigarette. Monica cast a suspicious glance at his synthetic black shirt, hesitated, then followed him into the bathroom, which now seemed to have established itself definitively as the scene of all profanation. He took a packet of Marlboros from the back pocket of his jeans, lit one, and started to puff out smoke with the confidence of a professional. He held the cigarette out to her and while the smoke swept over her face, he was struck by a mysterious sadness, shaking his head and declaring, 'What a shit party.'

From that day on, Lyonel decided they were a couple, or at least that they were doomed to maintain a relationship of a sexual nature. He started to send her letters in which he announced the erotic sensations she generated in him.

In a passionate style full of imagery, he revealed his desire to explore her anatomy or sniff her bodily fluids, and finished off with expressions such as: 'let me nibble your ear' or 'so long, baby'.

He phoned her several times a week, and overwhelmed by panic and the rules governing politeness, she always responded in an affable chirpy voice, swaying her head like a metronome to the rhythm of the slow dance music that he broadcast into the receiver. She felt as though her youth had strayed onto a deathly path, as if a mysterious anomaly was condemning her to vile mating rituals. He kissed her at the cinema when he took her to see *Dune*, and she let him do it, despite the disgust that this man disguised as a child roused in her and her dread that an acquaintance might suddenly appear. She looked dishevelled and was sweating almost as much as him.

After that, he stopped telephoning and writing to her. She started to watch out for the postman, with the feeling that she had experienced this scenario before, and, sure enough, once again the empty mailbox broke the news of her downfall. In the spring she bumped into him at a party, but he was laughing with a girl in a miniskirt and when she approached, he seemed to be staring at a point behind her. The following weekend, she decided to write to him at the address he had jotted down scrupulously on the envelopes containing his libidinous prose. She never imagined she would copy it out one day, forehead creased with anxiety. She asked him how he was, signed off with her first name and surname then added a PS in increasingly sloping handwriting: 'Is there a problem with the way I kiss, is that what it is?'

Three days later she found a message in the mailbox, in an envelope without a return address on the back. She tore open the envelope, apprehensive as if condemned, then discovering the red letters scrawled on a sheet of A4, was seized by the same dizziness as when she had inhaled smoke from their first Marlboro: 'Don't worry baby, your kiss = wow.'

Monica's personal diary,
1984–1986.

Despite all this, when they bumped into each other, he continued to ignore her, even when her development began to take a normal course and she had to buy herself a C-cup bra. He, on the other hand, did not really ever advance, so much so that until he took his baccalaureate he could always be found on the front row of class photos, crouching in the middle of a row of girls. It was an era of great change, as if a reversal of Earth's magnetic fields was being witnessed: those who had repelled the most attractive secondary school students started to magnetize them with mysterious force. While Lyonel's body refused to grow, his popularity ranking climbed dramatically. He began to go out with the prettiest girls in school, those who had intriguing reputations, like the one who had hitchhiked to Cadaques in northern Spain or another who had slept with a teaching assistant. Maybe the characters of the attractive blond boys whose names had been copied out endlessly the previous year had turned out to be disappointing. Hiding beneath their arrogant exteriors were all the qualities of frightened little girls.

On the other hand, Lyonel's constitution made the girls' cheeks burn like little hot plates: all those disturbing secretions and the thick hair they now imagined running their fingers through. But while other boys began to stare at Monica's backside in her jeans, Lyonel no longer looked at her.

That was when she began to suffer. At night in bed she started to reread his letters, and she developed a hopeless passion for him. Like a man susceptible to subtle charm, he had loved her tiny frame in her pleated skirt, but that biological time was over. She fancied him until she left school for good, taking stock of his conquests with a masochistic joy. She always considered him to be the archetypal gentleman, even years later when she bumped into him at a supermarket checkout, and he was fat and visibly drunk.

ALESSANDRO

In March 2001, Monica phoned an Italian TV station and asked to speak to Alessandro F.

She was passed from phone to phone, as if this man was as elusive in his professional life as he was elsewhere, jumping from office to office with a devilish indifference, but the call finally reached its intended destination. Monica revealed her personal status in one go, in a clear voice, administrative, without taking a breath. He said nothing, then pretended to be surprised, innocently shocked, and ended up by acknowledging the facts with a sigh of acceptance, like an armed robber who had been on the run for far too long.

She travelled to Milan to meet him, and a mixture of different feelings pervaded her, none of which seemed to fit the situation. She dressed as if she was going to a job interview, and whilst waiting for him in the hotel lobby, she remembered the frosty look her mother had given her when she announced that she wanted to get in touch with her biological father. 'Do what you want,' Ambra had said in a dismal tone, before opening the fridge and grabbing a bottle of beer, which no one had ever seen her do, not before that day or after.

He arrived on a Vespa scooter and, with his soft, bouncy hair and beige linen suit, looked like he was gearing up for a holiday fling.

He took her to a café in a square off via Andrea Maria Ampère and declared with convincing charm, 'There is electricity in the air.' From that moment on, nothing was accurately committed to Monica's memory. A cloud of mist seemed to erase the contours of reality as if they were spending the afternoon in a Turkish bath. The surrounding noises reached her ears as though she was submerged in magma, and the words exchanged between them, in a bizarre mixture of English, Italian and French, sounded as if they were being spoken in the depths of the ocean.

She bathed in a gentle euphoria, a state with all the treacherous warmth of carbon monoxide. She asked several questions about the romance between her mother and him, but he claimed he could remember nothing and instead preferred to discuss his family's claim to fame in hosting the kings of France since the fourteenth century. For a while they wandered through a labyrinth of streets, and whilst he searched in the shop windows for something he could buy her as a souvenir (a ball-point pen? stamps?), she experienced a sinking feeling, as though she was leaving the world of the living.

He was talkative, charming and recited old maxims in Latin which she nodded along to, smiling confidently and hopelessly. She had the docility of a captive, and when she mentioned her status as an illegitimate child, he gently lectured her, blaming her shameful tendency towards negativity. 'Just like Michelangelo or Leonardo da Vinci, but it didn't prevent them from doing great things.'

On returning to Paris, she received messages on her phone about her beauty or the cruelty of fate, messages that thrust her into an inappropriate state of agitation. Then, compelled to respond to the demands of his biological offspring, he recounted with remarkable literary rigour the story of his original sin with Ambra, claiming it was why he had been sent to this earth. He sent her his latest book, the title of which hinted at a life spent crushing the hearts of young girls, affectionate like kittens. He then changed his telephone number and failed to show further signs of life.

The Useless Seducer, *by Alessandro F, Lampi di Stampa.*

PART THREE

FALLING APART

THE END

Transcript of text messages.

8:13am, 12 September 2011, MS to XX.
Do you really think this is best?
I find it so sad. Personally, I've loved the last few months.
12:05pm, 12 September 2011, XX to MS.
I find it neither good nor bad.
Just sad but necessary and reasonable.
And I've loved the last few months as well.

précision. *Nébulosité d'une explication, d'une théorie.*
⇒ **confusion, flou, obscurité.** ◊ CONTR. Clarté, limpidité.

NÉCESSAIRE [nesesɛʀ] adj. et n. m. — XIIᵉ; lat. *necessarius*.
I. Adj. 1. Se dit d'une condition, d'un moyen dont la
présence ou l'action rend seule possible une fin ou un
effet. *Condition nécessaire et suffisante*¹ *pour qu'un
quadrilatère soit un rectangle* (ex. que deux de ses angles
successifs soient droits). *«Rabe ne possédait plus les deux
sous nécessaires afin de payer sa place»* (Mac Orlan). ⇒⇒⇒.
Il n'est pas nécessaire d'espérer pour entreprendre. **2.** Dont
l'existence, la présence est requise pour répondre au
besoin (de qqn), au fonctionnement (de qqch.).
⇒ **indispensable, utile.** NÉCESSAIRE À. *Les vitamines sont
nécessaires à l'organisme.* «*Voyez-vous, nos enfants nous
sont bien nécessaires*» (Hugo). ◊ ABSOL. Qui est très utile,
s'impose : dont on ne peut se passer. ⇒ **essentiel,
primordial.** «*Ils manquèrent de tout ce qui est nécessaire,
au milieu de tout ce qui est superflu*» (Diderot). *C'est un
mal nécessaire, que l'on tolère vu les avantages qu'il
comporte par ailleurs. Personne nécessaire* (par les
services qu'elle rend). «*La certitude d'être nécessaire
prolonge la vie des vieilles femmes*» (Mauriac). *Elle n'a pas
jugé nécessaire de nous prévenir*, elle ne nous a pas
prévenus et c'est regrettable. *Il est nécessaire d'en parler,
qu'on en dise un mot.* ⇒ **falloir** (il faut que). ◊◊ *Était-ce bien
nécessaire?* **3.** LOG. Qui est de la nature ou qui est l'effet
d'un lien logique, causal. *Enchaînement nécessaire d'un
effet par rapport à sa cause.* ⇒ **2. logique.** ⇒ — COUR. *Effet,
produit, résultat nécessaire, qui doit se produire imman-
quablement.* ⇒ **immanquable, inéluctable, inévitable,
infaillible, obligatoire, obligé.** «*toute chose humaine est
nécessaire et déterminée par la marche irrésistible de
l'ensemble des choses*» (Senancour). **4.** PHILOS. Qui existe
sans qu'il y ait de cause ni de condition à son existence.
⇒ **absolu, inconditionné, premier.** *L'Être nécessaire :* le Dieu
de Descartes, de Pascal.

NECESSARY:

1. Of a condition, of a process whereby its presence or action inevitably determines a result or effect.

It is not necessary to hope in order to undertake. (LOL)

2. That of which the existence or presence is required in order to respond to the need (of someone) or functioning (of someone).

That which one cannot do without.

A necessary evil.

3. That inevitably needs to happen. ⇒ **unmissable, unavoidable, inevitable, infallible, obligatory, required.**

4. That exists where there may not be a cause or condition to its existence. ⇒ **absolute, unconditioned, primary.**

RAISONNABLE [ʀɛzɔnabl] adj. — 1265 ; *reisnable* 1120 ; de raison* (voir l'encadré) **1.** DIDACT. Doué de raison. «*Le plaisir est l'objet, le devoir et le but De tous les êtres raisonnables*» (Voltaire). ⇒ **intelligent, pensant.** *L'homme, animal raisonnable.* ◊ (CHOSES) Conforme à la raison. ⇒ **rationnel.** «*La diversité de nos opinions ne vient pas de ce que les uns sont plus raisonnables que les autres*» (Descartes). **2.** COUR. Qui pense selon la raison, se conduit avec bon sens et mesure, d'une manière réfléchie. ⇒ **sensé.** *Un enfant raisonnable. Allons, soyez raisonnable, n'exigez pas l'impossible.* «*C'est toujours quand une femme se montre le plus résignée qu'elle paraît le plus raisonnable*» (Gide). ◊ (CHOSES) *Avis, opinion raisonnable. Interprétation raisonnable, fondée. Conduite, décision raisonnable.* ⇒ **judicieux, responsable, sage.** *Est-ce bien raisonnable?* — IMPERS. *Il est raisonnable de penser...* ⇒ **naturel, normal.** ◊ SPÉCIALT Qui consent des conditions honnêtes et modérées. *Commerçant, négociateur raisonnable.* **3.** Qui correspond à la mesure normale. *Accorder une liberté raisonnable à qqn. Prix raisonnable.* ⇒ **acceptable, modéré.** — *Assez important, au-dessus de la moyenne. Un raisonnable paquet d'actions.* «*Il était, quand je l'eus, de grosseur raisonnable*» (La Fontaine). ◊ CONTR. Déraisonnable, extravagant, fou, insensé, passionné, léger. Aberrant, absurde, illégitime, injuste; excessif, exorbitant.

REASONABLE:

Conforming to reason.

Thinking according to reason, behaving sensibly and in moderation, having a reflective manner.

It is always when a woman appears most resigned that she seems most reasonable (Gide).

ANT. Unreasonable, extravagant, mad: **passionate**, frivolous. Aberrant, absurd, unwarranted, unjust; excessive, exorbitant.

Necessary and reasonable: definitions from The Petit Robert, *dictionary of the French language (1967 edition).*

ANALYSIS OF VOCAB

NECESSARY	REASONABLE
EATING	BRUSHING YOUR TEETH
HOPING	GIVING UP
DARING	PREVENTING
SLEEPING	SLEEPING
ART	WORDS
(WRITING A BOOK)	(SEEING A SHRINK)
XX (HIM)	YY (SOMEONE ELSE)

DIAGRAM

Unprompted remarks collated following the break-up of MS with the loved one.

Guys (who don't know him).

— If that's the case, it's good news.
— Maybe you were just doing his head in.
— Make a fresh start.
— You need to sleep with another man as soon as possible.*
— A pretty girl like you . . . *
— He's an Italian? They are all chauvinists, the Italians.*
— Is he married?*
— Did he cheat on you?*
— Did he leave you for someone else?*
— Women can do anything in love. If a woman wants a man, she can have him.*
— It's like a ringroad: if it's jammed, you have to change your route. You have to adjust.*
— Personally, I've been with my wife for thirty years.*
— Maybe you've had a narrow escape.*
— What's you star sign? Aha, Leo! Leos aren't easy.*

*Comments made by taxi driver during a journey between Issy-les-Moulineaux and MS's home.

— In any case, what did you expect in this shitty place?*
— Six months, what's that on the geological time scale? Nothing.
Dust.

Guys (who know him).

— Let it go.
— Yes, but when you get to know him really well, he's a great guy.
— I knew his ex, she isn't bad.
— Fuck, drop it, life's too short.
— You're healthy, that's all that matters.
— He was in a film wasn't he?
— Last year in Cannes, it was a right laugh.

Girls (who don't know him).

— What a knob!
— His ex is irrelevant.
— Maybe he's scared.
— He doesn't feel up to it.
— Do you think he might be gay?
— You need to make an impression on him.
— Whatever, I don't understand blokes.
— I get the impression that all the nice girls I know are single.
— Don't take it the wrong way, but I think you're a masochist.

Girls (who know him).

— What a knob!
— He thinks the sun shines out of his arse, doesn't he?
— He's just not in your league.
— That guy doesn't love anyone but himself.
— In any case, in ten years' time he'll be bald.
— Are you joking?
— I didn't think that guy had a sex life.
— That moron with his leather jacket.
— Still, he's so laid back he's horizontal. He looks like he's on St John's wort.
— He could be France's youngest regional councillor (*referring to his dress sense*).
— That's a shame, he was sweet.

UNREST

Transcript of text messages between MS and XX, from 13 September to 14 November 2011.

8:02pm, 13 September 2011, MS to XX.
I thought it would be different with me.

8:08pm, 13 September 2011, XX to MS.
That's your crazy pride talking.

10:46pm, 22 September 2011, MS to XX.
Well there you go. I'm resigned to it.

10:47pm, 22 September, MS to XX.
Great, isn't it?

11:00pm, 22 September 2011, XX to MS.
I don't know.

11:05pm, 22 September 2011, MS to XX.
You have the right to have an opinion on things, you know.

11:18am, 24 September 2011, MS to XX.
I'm going to leave you a message. Please don't reply.

3:07pm, 24 September 2011, 15:07, XX to MS.
Without meaning to be arrogant, I also think I'm disappointing.

4:33am, 25 September 2011, MS to XX.
In fact I

10:12am, 26 September 2011, MS to XX.
You're in the process of losing me, you know.

11:58am, 26 September 2011, XX to MS.
But we've already lost each other.

12:42pm, 2 October 2011, XX to MS.
How are you doing?

12:42pm, 2 October 2011, MS to XX.
What the hell do you care?

5:39pm, 6 October 2011, MS to XX.
Do you want to meet up?

5:45pm, 6 October 2011, XX to MS.
I think I'd really like that, but it's up to you . . .

5:55pm, 6 October 2011, MS to XX.
It's complicated but let's do it.

6:00pm, 6 October 2011, XX to MS.
I'm leaving now. Tomorrow?

6:03pm, 6 October 2011, MS to XX.
OK, tomorrow.

11:06am, 7 October 2011, XX to MS.
Shall I take you for lunch?

11:07am, 7 October 2011, MS to XX.
I don't know really, lunches depress me.

11:08am, 7 October 2011, XX to MS.
OK, a coffee then, if you have a spare moment in the day?

11:21am, 7 October 2011, MS to XX.
Sorry, I think I'll have to pass.

4:48pm, 7 October 2011, MS to XX.
I have the urge for a cigarette.
Do you want to come for a smoke with me?

4:51pm, 7 October 2011, XX to MS.
Let's go.

5:50pm, 7 October 2011, XX to MS.
Thanks.

5:50pm, 7 October 2011, MS to XX.
What for?

7:18pm, 14 October 2011, MS to XX.
Are you thinking things over?

7:41pm, 14 October 2011, MS to XX.
OK. Very encouraging.

7:41pm, 14 October 2011, XX to MS.
Sorry, I couldn't get a signal in the basement where I was (perfect place for thinking things over).

11:42pm, 17 October 2011, MS to XX.
Thank you. Fuck, thank you.

11:50pm, 17 October 2011, MS to XX.
Well done, you're the man for the job!

12:26am, 18 October 2011, MS to XX.
You need to give me your secret for not giving a toss about anyone.

12:26am, 18 October 2011, XX to MS.
Let's say I do give a toss about something, what do you want me to reply to that comment?

10:03am, 19 October 2011, MS to XX.
I'm sorry, I know it's a bit heavy going.

1:52pm, 19 October 2011, XX to MS.
And I dare say you could really do without all this.

2:12am, 24 October 2011, MS to XX.
Are you asleep?

12:52pm, 26 October 2011, MS to XX.
If you keep ignoring my messages, I will kill the hostage (a multi-coloured stripy lighter).

12:54pm, 26 October 2011, XX to MS.
I knew it!

12:55pm, 26 October 2011, MS to XX.
Now we need to talk about the ransom. The kidnapper is waiting for an offer. Of a non-financial nature, of course.

2:12pm, 26 October 2011, MS to XX.
I want dinner.

2:12pm, 26 October 2011, XX to MS.
Is that the starting point for negotiation?

2:13pm, 26 October 2011, MS to XX.
A kidnapper with a life in her hands doesn't negotiate.

7:52pm, 26 October 2011, XX to MS.

Dalston Central Market: £3.

8:15pm, 26 October 2011, MS to XX.
Deal closed. The exchange will take place over dinner.

2:30pm, 30 October 2011, MS to XX.

2:32pm, 30 October 2011, MS to XX.
You will inform it that you've been to Corsica for the weekend.

3:57pm, 30 October 2011, XX to MS.

11:11pm, 14 November 2011, MS to XX.
No heart, no balls, no class.

STAR SYSTEM

Extract from a promo interview with David Lynch, carried out by MS at Silencio, rue Montmartre, Paris II, 29 August 2011.

'At university I had two girlfriends, one was secret. She was the one I loved. One day, I invited her to lunch and I asked her if she loved me. She replied . . . *(whispering)* "no" . . . Oh! It was hard . . . After that, I thought about her for twenty years. She returned incessantly in my dreams. Even during my marriages. How many times have I been married? . . . Four, that's right. Well, during my four marriages, I carried on dreaming about her. But, you know, she did love me. Some years later, she told me. She just hadn't realized it at that point. One day, a while back, I decided to call her. And you know what? The second I heard her voice *(he clicks his fingers)*, at that very second, it was all over. Freedom. *(silence)*. Would you like a tissue? The things you imagine are much more beautiful than reality, you understand, don't you?'

At 7:15pm on 1 September 2011, MS called XX.
On hearing his voice, she hung up.
She experienced no feeling of freedom.

THE MIRACLE

29 November 2011, MS bumped into XX in the lift at work. He raised a hand towards her and adjusted a button on her cardigan. After work, he offered her a lift on his scooter.

Grey Isabel Marant cardigan, equipped with magic powers.

THE ENIGMA

Email sent by MS to XX.
1:29pm, 1 December 2011. Extract.

There's one thing I don't understand: why did you spend the night with me, if what you feel for me is so obvious? This is a real question, I'm lost. Yesterday you seemed so indifferent.

Email sent by XX to MS.
2:47pm, 1 December 2011.

Response. The night: because in the spur of the moment and with the promise of one night together without repercussions, and faced with such confident desire from you, foolishly, I desired it too. What you felt as indifference: my own feelings suppressed in response to the insistence of the expression of yours. You tell me you don't understand me, that you find me confusing, so I make an effort to be clear and to the point. But most of all, I don't want to be cruel to you, and if you feel that I am, I'm sorry about that.

THE BAIT

Grey tops worn by MS between 5 December 2011 and 1 March 2012,
in the hope of physical contact with XX.
(Sexual relations between MS and XX between 5 December 2011
and 1 March 2012: none.)

DEATH

Email sent by MS to Ambra P.
11:29pm, 30 January 2012. Extract.

Mum,
You asked me what you could do to make me 'feel better'. Well you could, for example, tell me what you felt when Alessandro left you. I might possibly feel better after that.

Email sent by Ambra P to MS.
9:12am, 31 January 2012. Extract.

Sweetheart,
I'm sorry to hear that you haven't managed to pull through. I don't really remember as I was so young when I was with Alessandro. I guess I felt sad, of course, but as anyone would after a break-up.
Big hugs, sweetheart.

YVES

It was December 1972 when Ambra first met Yves S in a ski resort in Switzerland. She breezed around like a wealthy heiress without a care in the world. They had been seated next to each other at dinner, most likely in the hope they would get together, but not a glance came her way. Back then she still had long blonde hair and a tormented look about her that made some men want to lock her away, forever. Apart from Yves S, it seemed. He thrust his carnivorous little teeth into the red meat in front of him and smiled at the excessively tanned Brazilian girl opposite. He captivated women with his smile and intellectual banter, exuding an uneasy charm, a sort of erotic intimidation. He worked at the United Nations in Geneva, and whilst no one really understood what his job at the International Labour Office entailed, the diplomatic corps number plate on his Mercedes certainly evoked a fascinating world of muffled negotiations.

According to 'legend', the Brazilian turned down his offer of an escort home, and their fate was sealed. Yves S removed his glasses, turned towards the ethereal blonde next to him who was putting on her ski hat and said, rather like a domineering father: 'Up! Come on. Let's go.'

They got married on 4 August 1973 in the hotel gardens of La Réserve by Lake Léman, Geneva. That same day, Yves S became

Monica's legal guardian. The need to move to Switzerland had been explained to her quite simply with an indisputable line of reasoning: 'This is your dad.'

Curiously, the little girl does not appear in the wedding photos, while the images of her mother's long emerald dress create a strange optical illusion, as though her outfit is blending into the green lawn. Guests were thin on the ground and virtually all elderly, which was almost as depressing as Yves's smile. And when he took off his glasses his melancholy became even more apparent, as did his squinty eye.

Ambra came to the conclusion that the photos were disastrous and drew flowers and multicoloured balloons on every page of the wedding album. On the photo taken at the Town Hall, she stuck a picture of a gun pointing at Yves S's head. Monica often flicked through the album with an uneasy fascination. She also studied her mother's many Indian ink drawings for a long, long time, especially the one that showed her new father in tails, smiling and casually leaning against a wall, brandishing a bloody axe and the bride's veil.

Ambra and Yves S: the wedding album, 1973.

MONICA (PART 3)

Monica adapted to her new life with the flexibility and good will of a child, especially one born in sin. Several months after she arrived in Geneva, she was speaking French and had altogether stopped speaking Italian, a language born of a world that no longer existed to her, like the city of Pompeii, buried and paralysed beneath the ashes and pumice. In August 1974, she joyfully welcomed her brother Fabrice into the world, and, carefree, bounded into the unknown territory of nursery school as if she were being sent away purely due to her own desire for freedom.

In November 1974, Monica climbed onto a slide at Bertrand Park, and with her mother looking on she dived headfirst onto the concrete. She broke her nose, and for several weeks her face was so swollen that it made everyone feel uncomfortable, but that did not stop her from smiling like a politician principally concerned about the well-being of her electorate.

From that day on, she made remarkably regular trips to A&E and the paediatrician. It was as if the slide episode had revealed a secret urge to tumble and fall. In fact it happened incessantly, in the street, park, nursery, at school. Falling apart in an unassuming way, silently, but in a very distinctive manner: always falling headfirst, without ever using her hands for protection.

It was Monica's personal hallmark and it was responsible for some impressive wounds including giant bumps on her forehead, black eyes, a bloody chin, gashed cheeks, and the acrobatic pinnacle of it all, a head injury sustained by falling off a stationary bicycle with stabilizers. She practised this skilful art until 1977, when she was forced to take up judo.

There she came to face to face with Mr Weber, a German-speaking Swiss teacher who did not mess around when it came to issues of coordination. So, Monica had to stop expressing her creativity by means of trauma, and finally defeated, she picked up her yellow belt.

Monica, 1975.

THE WOUND

11:45pm, 20 February 2012. The following words were spoken by Anna C in the presence of MS, in an apartment in the 10th arrondissement of Paris.

'I was at Laurence's place on Saturday . . . XX was there with his girlfriend . . . You know, Constance, she works in the film industry.'

10:20am, 23 February 2012. MS tripped over the kerb.

Medical Imaging and
Examination Centre
80, rue de Rennes
75006 Paris

25/02/12

Reference: AB/DP

Madame MS

Dr Denis Solignac
X-ray of the left foot

Indication: localized trauma (dosimetry: PDS: 11.7cGy/cm^2).

Diagnosis: undisplaced fracture of the base of the fifth metatarsal.

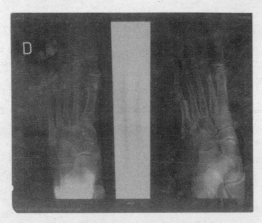

X-ray of MS's left foot, February 2012.

L'Express *magazine featuring the article:*
'Narcissistic Perverts: How to recognize them', embezzled by MS from the
waiting room of the Medical Imaging and Examination Centre.

DEATH (PART 2)

Transcript of text messages.

9:02pm, 27 February, MS to XX.
My fault, I didn't think a drink would be so difficult. Sorry.

9:15pm, 27 February, MS to XX.
Are you annoyed?

9:20pm, 27 February, XX to MS.
No, of course not.

10:02pm, 27 February, MS to XX.
Without you, I just can't do it. I CAN'T DO IT.

11:24pm, 27 February, XX to MS.
I'm afraid that has nothing to do with me.

3:03pm, 3 March 2012. Email sent by MS (work account) to MS (private account).

Ican'tdoitIcan'tdoitIcan'tdoitIcan'tdoitIcan'tdoitIcan'tdoit-
Ican'tdoitIcan'tdoitIcan'tdoitIcan'tdoitIcan'tdoitIcan'tdoit-
Ican'tdoitIcan'tdoitIcan'tdoitIcan'tdoitIcan'tdoitIcan'tdoit-
Ican'tdoitIcan'tdoitIcan'tdoitIcan'tdoitIcan'tdoitIcan'tdoit-
Ican'tdoitIcan'tdoitIcan'tdoitIcan'tdoitIcan'tdoitIcan'tdoit-
Ican'tdoitIcan'tdoitIcan'tdoitIcan'tdoitIcan'tdoitIcan'tdoit-
Ican'tdoitIcan'tdoitIcan'tdoitIcan'tdoitIcan'tdoitIcan'tdoit-
Ican'tdoitIcan'tdoitIcan'tdoitIcan'tdoitIcan'tdoitIcan'tdoit-
Ican'tdoitIcan'tdoitIcan'tdoitIcan'tdoitIcan'tdoitIcan'tdoit-
Ican'tdoitIcan'tdoitIcan'tdoitIcan'tdoitIcan'tdoitIcan'tdoit-
Ican'tdoitIcan'tdoitIcan'tdoitIcan'tdoitIcan'tdoitIcan'tdoit-
Ican'tdoitIcan'tdoitIcan'tdoitIcan'tdoitIcan'tdoitIcan'tdoit-
Ican'tdoitIcan'tdoitIcan'tdoitIcan'tdoitIcan'tdoitIcan'tdoit-
Ican'tdoitIcan'tdoitIcan'tdoitIcan'tdoitIcan'tdoitIcan'tdoit-
Ican'tdoitIcan'tdoitIcan'tdoitIcan'tdoitIcan'tdoitIcan'tdoit-
Ican'tdoitIcan'tdoitIcan'tdoitIcan'tdoitIcan'tdoitIcan'tdoit-
Ican'tdoitIcan'tdoitIcan'tdoitIcan'tdoitIcan'tdoitIcan'tdoit-
Ican'tdoitIcan'tdoitIcan'tdoitIcan'tdoitIcan'tdoitIcan'tdoit-
Ican'tdoitIcan'tdoitIcan'tdoitIcan'tdoitIcan'tdoitIcan'tdoit-
Ican'tdoitIcan'tdoitIcan'tdoitIcan'tdoitIcan'tdoitIcan'tdoit-
Ican'tdoitIcan'tdoitIcan'tdoitIcan'tdoitIcan'tdoitIcan'tdoit-
Ican'tdoitIcan'tdoitIcan'tdoitIcan'tdoitIcan'tdoitIcan'tdoit-
Ican'tdoitIcan'tdoitIcan'tdoitIcan'tdoitIcan'tdoitIcan'tdoit-
Ican'tdoitIcan'tdoitIcan'tdoitIcan'tdoitIcan'tdoitIcan'tdoit-
Ican'tdoitIcan'tdoitIcan'tdoitIcan'tdoitIcan'tdoitIcan'tdoit-

Ican'tdoitIcan'tdoitIcan'tdoitIcan'tdoitIcan'tdoitIcan'tdoit-
Ican'tdoitIcan'tdoitIcan'tdoitIcan'tdoitIcan'tdoitIcan'tdoit-
Ican'tdoitIcan'tdoitIcan'tdoitIcan'tdoitIcan'tdoitIcan'tdoit-
Ican'tdoitIcan'tdoitIcan'tdoitIcan'tdoitIcan'tdoitIcan'tdoit-
Ican'tdoitIcan'tdoitIcan'tdoitIcan'tdoitIcan'tdoitIcan'tdoit-
Ican'tdoitIcan'tdoitIcan'tdoitIcan'tdoitIcan'tdoitIcan'tdoit
Ican'tdoitIcan'tdoitIcan'tdoitIcan'tdoitIcan'tdoitIcan'tdoit-
Ican'tdoitIcan'tdoitIcan'tdoitIcan'tdoitIcan'tdoitIcan'tdoit-
Ican'tdoitIcan'tdoitIcan'tdoitIcan'tdoitIcan'tdoitIcan'tdoit-
Ican'tdoitIcan'tdoitIcan'tdoitIcan'tdoitIcan'tdoitIcan'tdoit-
Ican'tdoitIcan'tdoitIcan'tdoitIcan'tdoitIcan'tdoitIcan'tdoit-
Ican'tdoitIcan'tdoitIcan'tdoitIcan'tdoitIcan'tdoitIcan'tdoit-
Ican'tdoitIcan'tdoitIcan'tdoitIcan'tdoitIcan'tdoitIcan'tdoit-
Ican'tdoitIcan'tdoitIcan'tdoitIcan'tdoitIcan'tdoitIcan'tdoit-
Ican'tdoitIcan'tdoitIcan'tdoitIcan'tdoitIcan'tdoitIcan'tdoit-
Ican'tdoitIcan'tdoitIcan'tdoitIcan'tdoitIcan'tdoitIcan'tdoit-
Ican'tdoitIcan'tdoitIcan'tdoitIcan'tdoitIcan'tdoitIcan'tdoit-
Ican'tdoitIcan'tdoitIcan'tdoitIcan'tdoitIcan'tdoitIcan'tdoit
Ican'tdoitIcan'tdoitIcan'tdoitIcan'tdoitIcan'tdoitIcan'tdoit-
Ican'tdoitIcan'tdoitIcan'tdoitIcan'tdoitIcan'tdoitIcan'tdoit-
Ican'tdoitIcan'tdoitIcan'tdoitIcan'tdoitIcan'tdoitIcan'tdoit-
Ican'tdoitIcan'tdoitIcan'tdoitIcan'tdoitIcan'tdoitIcan'tdoit-
Ican'tdoitIcan'tdoitIcan'tdoitIcan'tdoitIcan'tdoitIcan'tdoit-
Ican'tdoitIcan'tdoitIcan'tdoitIcan'tdoitIcan'tdoitIcan'tdoit

NICOLE

It was December 1985 when Monica realized she was unbalanced, and that most likely her destiny lay in prostitution. She was spending her holidays on the Côte d'Azur with her family and her American penpal, Nicole, a blonde with a ponytail whose sorry smile concealed a pathological obsession with pornography.

The past year had been a tumultuous one. There had been parties at home, lots of parties, where her mother would dress up as a saloon girl or a slave wearing a metal neck chain, leaving traces of red lipstick around the rims of champagne cocktail glasses. There had also been silence, a pleasant but disturbing silence that fell like snow in the weeks leading up to the first 'maternal evacuation'. Then one morning Ambra got up, pulled on some jeans, and driven by a dark force that compelled her to abandon the world in general and domestic life in particular, she took to the wheel of her scruffy old hatchback. Her road trip ended in a psychiatric clinic on the edge of Lake Léman, a place that worked wonders with the imagination, for it was forbidden to visit her or even speak to her on the telephone, as if she were in training at some secret service location.

When she returned home, there was no real evidence to say what she had been up to on her little trip, apart from the fact that she chucked all the cheap ashtrays in the bin. Family life returned to normal, and her other existence, impalpable like the shadow of an illusion, was never even mentioned.

That winter, Christmas was spent in Cap d'Antibes, in a hotel over-looking the sea, a place of excessive white marble and abandoned deckchairs that emitted a morbid sadness.

Nicole had flown over from Rhode Island with the firm intention of mastering the French art of love. She smoked at the window every evening, waiting till midnight when, at that precise time, she would sidle down the corridor wearing a miniskirt and irresistible perfume and disappear until the early hours of the morning. For the first few days, Monica watched these antics with a mixture of alarm and amazement. Providence never ceased to remind her that she could rely on nothing and no one. But mostly, she just felt excluded again when she wanted to be part of the action. It was like everything was happening far from her gaze and all that remained was anxious contemplation as she waited to experience the thrills of womanhood.

For the first few days, she stood watching at the window with a wilted smile, following the fragile figure of Nicole as she evaporated into the darkness.

During the day, Monica watched in admiration as Nicole, this duplicitous young woman in a tennis outfit, fooled everyone around her. She was wonderfully polite, even a little reserved, and nothing hinted at her succubian night-time alter ego, apart from the menacing looks she gave Frank, the barman from Cannes: she had already demonstrated for him the meaning of the term 'blowjob'.

On Christmas Eve, Monica decided it was time to live dangerously. Throughout the day, she had felt a sort of intense excitement, the impatience mixed with relief that usually precedes the final accomplishment of a dangerous endeavour. At midnight, she trailed behind Nicole, walking through the revolving door of the hotel lobby and straight into a car outside that stank of sweat, tobacco and ham sandwiches. Once Monica was inside, the car door slammed shut, and she planted her forehead against the steamy window, watching the moving shapes outside dissolve into the distance as if they were swimming in an aquarium.

She spent the evening with Jeff, an Australian surfer, twenty-two years old, and huge at six foot three. When she was with him it looked like he was having an inappropriate relationship with a child. However, he was strangely devoid of sexual drive, as if his brain was a different age to his other more prominent organs. Or perhaps practising a sport in the open air had drained his body of all erotic desire. He put his arm around her shoulder in the car and that was the one and only indication of sexual conquest.

On New Year's Eve, Yves S surprised Monica and Jeff at two o'clock in the morning as they sat on the wet sand, surrounded by incriminating evidence of sin and depravation – packets of cigarettes, bottles of beer and a bath towel.

Nicole had altered her modus operandi, and was now satisfying her appetite for French culture in the bedroom she shared with Monica, where members of the local community were made very welcome each evening. Whilst that was going on, Monica wandered along the beach in the humid evening air. Jeff accompanied her, gathering up fragments of shell, explaining in detail the different species of snakes in the Australian outback, or politely and half-heartedly pecking her on the lips.

Monica sometimes played with the buckle on his belt, or slid her hand under his jumper, but Jeff did not seem to notice, preferring instead to run his fingers through her hair and rearrange her side parting.

But it seemed that Yves S was unaware that they had the non-existent sex life of an elderly couple, or hippies who only make love to nature. The following week, he stopped speaking to Monica, who continued to slowly turn into a ghost gliding along the corridors of the hotel, whilst Nicole played tennis with Ambra.

Back in Geneva a few weeks later she received a letter from Jeff – mostly talking about his journey home to Alice Springs and getting bronchitis – and Yves S called her a whore and said she was going to end up 'being screwed by everything that moved'. Monica was banned from going out until the following summer, when she was sent to spend three weeks with Nicole in Providence, Rhode Island. There she was greeted by a family that was as distant as her own, although a little more friendly, and she was able to connect once more with the warmth of another human being. She was almost happy there, especially during the calm summer nights spent watching X-rated films, snuggled up to Nicole, who stared at the screen whilst softly stroking her arm with an innocent little smile on her face.

YVES (PART 2)

One Wednesday evening in October 1989, Ambra packed a few T-shirts in an overnight bag, put her hair in a ponytail for the first time in nineteen years, and acting as if she were living in another dimension where she was unaware of her children's questions ('Are you going on holiday?'), she left the marital home for ever. Later, she claimed that if Yves S had not turned round and said to the kids, 'No, the whore's clearing off,' she probably would have unpacked her bag and prepared the dinner.

Life had taken one of those unexpected turns. That evening, Yves S drove around aimlessly in the scruffy hatchback with the fugitive's opera cassettes and glasses sat imposingly on the dashboard. He searched for her in the darkness, staring intently out of the windscreen, his jaw clenched. It is hard to know what his reaction would have been if the pale, ghostly figure of Ambra suddenly materialized in the headlights. Would he have dashed over to her, held her in his arms, breathing in the scent of her hair? Would he have grabbed her by the arm and thrown her into the passenger seat like a mere object of his possession? Would he have killed her in the middle of the street, leaving her body to slowly tumble to the pavement, discarded somewhere between a streetlight and a post box?

In the weeks that followed, Yves S started to drink whisky in huge tumblers. He had brought them back from the US and they could hold an entire 50cl bottle of Coke.

Now and again, Ambra phoned her children, but her voice was a distant murmur, as if the phone line did not quite reach to where she was. And the conversations were always the same: brief, strained. 'Come and get us, Dad's gone crazy,' Monica would say, and then Yves S would suddenly appear in the room, hurl himself at the phone and the line would go dead. Ambra tried her hardest not to give away even the slightest clue to her location. Perhaps she was in the Southern Hemisphere, or perhaps in a phone box on the corner of the street.

In December, Monica stopped thinking of Ambra as someone she could talk to. From then on, she felt as though the shadow cast over her head now swept across the whole apartment, crawling up the walls like something unsavoury, a sign of contamination, condemning its occupants to isolation. In the evening, Yves S played French billiards in the lounge, a tumbler by his side, whilst Fabrice eviscerated his mattress with a Japanese sword (no one ever knew how he acquired it).

Later that month, Ambra phoned to let them know she had moved to Carouge, a bohemian district of Geneva where she had rented a studio apartment, an apartment where Yves S would smash in the door on Christmas Eve, then try to strangle her before she retaliated, ramming a pair of scissors into the palm of his left hand.

Yves S and Ambra, Prohibition party,
December 1986.

YVES (PART 3)

In the first few years after they met, Monica and Yves had an affectionate relationship, so much so that they were often mistaken for a real father and daughter. Everyone had forgotten how they first came together, even those who had met the pale, blonde little girl as she clung to her mother when Yves S had first introduced his Italian fiancée just a few months earlier. Monica's absence at their wedding ceremony seemed as natural as her presence in the heart of the home the very next day. It was as if, overnight, Ambra and Yves S had fast-forwarded their lives together.

Between 1973 and 1978, Yves S took Monica's photo at every significant place or point in her life (park, fairground, Christmas), a preoccupation that filled a collection of albums entitled Monica 1, 2, 3 and 4. In 1977, he framed her first work of fiction, entitled *Today I Travelled to the Moon*, which described the modern-day solitude of a female explorer who encounters extra-terrestrial beings. Between 1979 and 1982, they watched every film starring Ginger Rogers and Fred Astaire. And whenever they decided to watch *Singin' in the Rain* on video, it was only so they could discuss Gene Kelly's obvious shortcomings. Yves S signed her school reports and Ambra liked to say that Monica had 'her father's intelligence'. (*But who was she talking about?*)

In 1979, he bought her an aquarium. Whilst Ambra slowly melted away as if she were leading a liquid existence, every weekend Yves S would accompany Monica to the pet shop, where they chose new species of fish. They entered the shop as if it were another world, inhaling the air infused with odours of the wild. Excitedly, beneath the cries of equatorial birds, they pushed their noses right up against the steamy glass of the aquariums.

THE ABYSS

In the winter of 1990, a hidden memory came flooding back, striking the surface of Monica's consciousness, long after the tank had been put out with the rubbish, coated in mould and mildew. Like a bubble floating upwards from the depths of the sea, slowly, very slowly, sweetly fragile but poisoned, images of a daily secret emerged. A stifled explosion, an aquarium lit up at night, fish gliding through algae and Yves S's hand inside her nightdress.

SORROW

Medical Imaging and
Examination Centre
80, rue de Rennes
75006 Paris

19/03/12

Reference: AB/DP
Madame MS
Dr Solignac

X-ray of the lungs.
Indication: pneumothorax
Diagnosis: bronchopneumonia of the right lung.

NB: Internal causes of illness (Nei Yin) are essentially of an
emotional nature. Five basic emotions can affect the body
when they are out of balance, and each one of them is
associated with a particular organ. Sadness (Yu) is associated
with the lungs.
(Extract from *The Treatise of Chinese Medicine: Acupuncture,
Moxas, Massage, Bloodletting*, edited by Dr A. Chamfrault,
published by Editions Coquemard.)

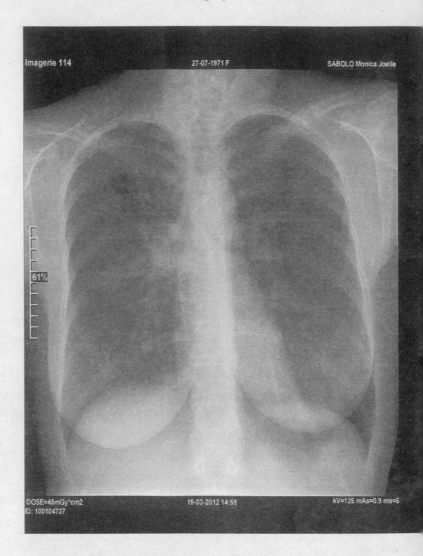

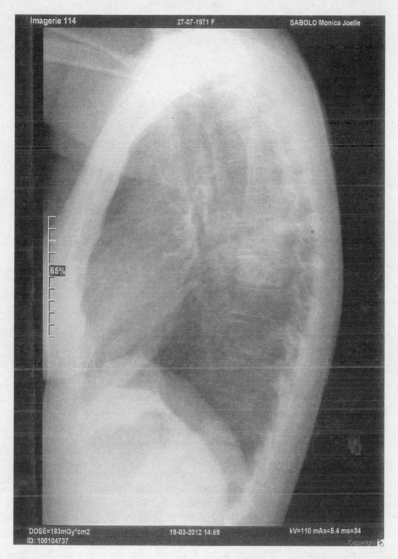

X-ray of MS's right lung, March 2012.

DRUGS

Medication and food supplements taken by MS in March and April 2012.

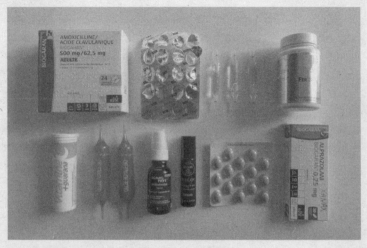

Alprazolam (Xanax), 0.25mg.
Amoxicillin antibiotics/Biogaran clavulanic acid, 500mg/62.5mg.
Organic Royal Jelly, 15ml vials.
Manganese-Copper-Oligosol, 2ml vials.
Omegabiane DHA, rich in Omega 3.
Magnesium with vitamin B6.
Stress roll-on, with original Bach flowers and essential oils, elixirs etc.
Somniphyt melatonin spray, sleep within easy reach.
Vitamin C + guarana, boosts energy, chewable tablets.
Iron, Vitall+, 27mg.

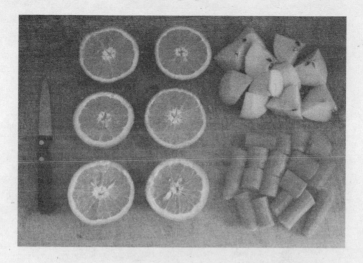

Pieces of orange, carrot and apple.

HELPLESSNESS

Copy of a note written by MS in April 2012.

'What I'm able to do:
– Eat
– Drink
– Smoke
– Get dressed
– Leave the house (before nightfall) (not every day)
– Write (not every day).'

DOES THIS SCOOTER BELONG TO XX?

Photos taken by MS in February 2012.

Photos taken by MS in April 2012.

Relapse: Cannes Film Festival.
Photos taken by MS in May 2012.

Photos taken by MS in September 2012.

LOVE

Objects donated to MS for comfort.

Miraculous medal. Donated by Sister Claire-Emmanuelle.

Burkina Faso fetish mask for purification rituals. Donated by Tifenn D.

Native American dreamcatcher. Donated by Florence W.

Grey cotton T-shirt from Propr Clothing (with superior magic powers). Donated by Adrienne T.

André Rieu Fiesta! *CD. Donated by Charlotte R.*

Sachet of White Widow weed from the Netherlands. Donated by Victor D.

Cola-flavoured Chupa Chups lolly. Donated by Franck V

Chanel Rouge Allure Lipstick, No. 18: Sexy. Donated by Bénédicte G.

Picnic: A Breath of Fresh Air *LP, released by EMI Harvest. Donated by Alexandra M.*

Gold ring. Donated by Sarah DB..

Cactus from Guatemala. In flower, needs no care. Donated by Erick G.

Light therapy lamp. Donated by Tifenn D, Dorian D, Côme MK, Sophie P, Claire T and Florence W.

Books donated to MS for comfort.

Simple Passion *by Annie Ernaux, Gallimard. Donated by Aurélia P.*

Think Like a Champion *by Donald Trump, Running Press. Donated by Florence W.*

Exquisite Pain *by Sophie Calle, Actes Sud. Donated by Emmanuelle L*

The Passion of Christ According to the French Baroque Poets, *Orphée, la Différence. Donated by Dorothée JG.*

He's Just Not That Into You *by Greg Behrendt and Liz Tuccillo, Harper Element. Donated by Adrian I.*

Love is a Dog from Hell *by Charles Bukowski, Grasset. Donated by Yann LP.*

Unhappy Love Affair *by Jean-Edern Hallier, Hallier. Donated by Côme MK.*

The End of the Story *by Lydia Davis, Phébus. Donated by Valentine F.*

Kiss & Tell: A Romantic Résumé, Ages 0 to 22 *by MariNaomi, Harper Perennial. Donated by Sophie P.*

Lili is Disappointed in Love *by Dominique de Saint Mars and Serge Bloch, Aligram. Donated by Julia B.*

The Gospel of St Matthew, *Bayard. Donated by the Archdiocese of Avignon*

The Good-for-Nothing *by Marcel Aymé, Gallimard. Donated by Aline G.*

The Weight of Secrets *by Aki Shimazaki, boxset of five books, Babel, Actes Sud.*
Confusion *by Stefan Zweig, Stock.*
The Wasted Vigil *by Nadeem Aslam, Seuil.*
The Room *by Hubert Selby Jr, 10/18.*
This Book Will Save Your Life *by A. M. Homes, Actes Sud.*
Life is Elsewhere *by Milan Kundera, Folio.*
Everything Good Will Come *by Sefi Atta, Babel, Actes Sud.*
Freedom *by Jonathan Franzen, L'Olivier.*
Collection donated by Tifenn D.

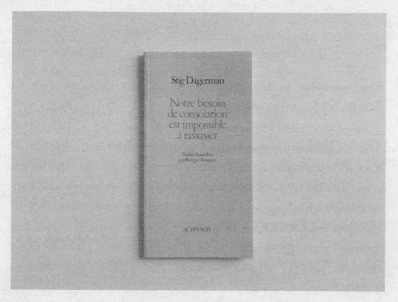

Our Need for Consolation Is Insatiable *by Stig Dagerman, Actes Sud. Donated by XX.*

FRANZISKA

One Thursday in December 2012, Monica attended Yves S's funeral in Lausanne, Switzerland.

The day was like a battle under water, somewhere at the bottom of a cold, translucent lake. When she was spoken to, the words reminded her of a strange song, a blend of raspy breath and low-frequency whistling, as if she were swimming amongst whales, in the open sea, far, very far, from shore. The guests moved around as a group, with supple and synchronized movements, rather like a shoal of sardines, their eyes beady. 'Your father was someone extraordinary.'

The priest offered a prayer to the congregation in a steady, confident voice, as if the life of Yves S had not been an enigma. Then Monica's brother Fabrice said a few words at the lectern. 'We all loved him,' he declared.

The ceremony was held in a basement room that felt like a sterile vault, and at the end when men in black were silently approaching, Franziska, Yves S's latest wife, suddenly dashed forward. Looking both agile and rabid, she leapt up, throwing herself onto the raised coffin and in a youthful, romantic, wild gesture, tore a fabric rose from the display of flowers attached to its side.

Monica watched Franziska, the flower she was gripping, solace and keepsake, remains of a past that lay right there, close by, at the bottom of a box. In the synthetic, derisory and everlasting petals, love throbbed like a heart ripped in two. At that exact moment, Monica's lungs filled up, swiftly, and she felt as if she was being propelled towards the surface, to the freedom of the open air.

Monica holding a dragonfly, 1977.

picador.com

blog
videos
interviews
extracts